FAVOURITE Bedtime STORIES

An illustrated treasury

FAVOURITE Bedtime STORIES

An illustrated treasury

LITTLE TIGER

LONDON

Contents

Spike The Softy

Written by Amelia Hepworth

Illustrated by Richard Watson

Spike The Softy

Charlie was a very lucky boy who had lots and lots of toys. Big toys, small toys, fluffy toys and . . . *spiky* toys. Well, just one spiky toy – SPIKE! Spike was a dinosaur. He had scaly green skin, a toothy grin and lots of purple spikes.

"I'm Spike!" boasted Spike. "I'm rough and I'm tough and I'm spiky all over. Spike by name and spiky by nature!"

While the other toys were busy playing tea parties, Spike played a very important game of Knights and Dragons with Charlie. Together they practised their scariest roars, battled enormous monsters, and rescued princesses from dragons. And by bedtime Spike was really quite worn out.

The other toys were all bathed and ready for bed by the time Spike got home from his adventure.

"I can't wait for my kiss goodnight," sighed Bunny, sleepily. All the other toys nodded happily – they were looking forward to snuggling up in bed together, just like always.

Spike rolled his beady eyes. After all, why would a rough, tough, spiky dinosaur need kisses or cuddles, or bedtime snuggles?

"Time for bed now, Charlie!" called Charlie's mum from downstairs. Charlie gathered all his toys and scrambled into bed. But he had been growing bigger and bigger every day and it was *such* a squash! There was barely room for Charlie!

"This is getting silly!" said Mum, when she came to tuck him in. "From now on you can only take one toy to bed with you."

"But Muuuuuuuuummmm!" cried Charlie.

"No 'buts', Charlie. Now who are you going to choose?" asked Mum, gently. Every toy held their breath to see who would be chosen. Every toy except Spike that is.

"I think I'll choose . . . Big Ted," said Charlie at last, "because he's good to snuggle up with." The other toys sighed with disappointment.

"I'm sure he'll pick someone else tomorrow," said Suzie (she was a very sensible doll).

"Well I don't mind if I don't get picked!" announced Spike bravely. "Bedtime cuddles are for softies. And I'm rough and I'm tough and I'm . . ."

". . . spiky all over. Yes, we know, Spike," said Bunny, kindly. "But if you did want to snuggle up with the rest of us tonight, you'd be very welcome."

But Spike had already stomped off to find himself somewhere else to sleep, alone.

The next night Charlie *did* pick someone else.
He picked Bunny, because she was squidgy and
she smelled good.

And after that,
Charlie picked
Patch with his
soft tummy.

Then Suzie with her fluffy hair.

But not Spike.

Spike didn't mind of course. Not one bit. Well . . . maybe he minded a little. In fact, as he watched Charlie snuggle up in bed without him for yet another night, Spike wondered if being rough and tough wasn't actually such a good thing. After all, who would want to snuggle up with someone so spiky? No one, that's who.

"Oh, oh, I'll *never* get a bedtime cuddle *ever* again," he thought, sadly. And as the other toys settled down to sleep, a single fat tear rolled down Spike's scaly, green face, and landed PLOP! in front of him.

But just then, there was a knock at the bedroom door. "Who's there?" whispered Charlie into the darkness. It was his little sister, Anna.

"There's a m-m-m-m-m-m-monster!" wailed Anna, in tears. "And he's hiding under my bed!"

Charlie sighed. *He* knew there was no such thing as monsters under the bed, but Anna was only little. "Would you like to read a story, Anna?" he asked.

"Yes please!" she smiled. So Anna snuggled up with her brother and they read her favourite story together until her head began to nod, and her eyes started to close.

"I think it's time you went back to bed," said Charlie, seriously. His mum had told him he must be a good big brother to his sister.

"But who will protect me from the monster?" asked Anna in a small voice. She looked like she might cry again.

Charlie thought about this for a moment. "I know!" he laughed. "You need Spike! No monster's a match for the roughest, toughest, spikiest dinosaur in all the land."

"That's me!" thought Spike in delight. "Charlie's talking about me! I'll protect Anna from the monster!" And he flashed his toothy grin, puffed up his purple spikes and his scaly chest swelled with pride.

So Charlie tucked Anna and Spike into bed together and gave them both a big kiss. It was a bit of a squash but Spike didn't mind one bit. In fact, don't tell anyone, but he enjoyed his bedtime cuddle very much indeed. And as he nodded off, Spike thought how maybe, just maybe, he could get to like being rough and tough . . . and a softy inside.

Bear Can't Sleep!

Written by Juliet Groom

Illustrated by Natasha Rimmington

Bear Can't Sleep!

It was late at night, and deep in Tall Tree Forest everyone was asleep.

Everyone, that is, except for Bear. His big comfy bed was cosy and warm.

The glow from Mouse's night-light twinkled softly on the ceiling of their

cave. But Bear was not even a little bit sleepy.

 Over in his small comfy bed, Mouse was asleep and dreaming with

a gentle *psssh-pssh-pssh*. And as Bear listened to Mouse snoring he gave

a big sigh.

"Maybe a sip of water will help," thought Bear, padding to the sink. But a drink didn't make him sleepy. Neither did counting sheep. And as Bear lay wide awake in his bed, all he could think about was Mouse, fast asleep across the room. *Psssh-pssh-pssh-pssh.*

"How very annoying of Mouse to sleep so very well when I'm awake," Bear harrumphed to himself. "I'm sure that if Mouse couldn't sleep I would stay up to talk to him."

Bear tossed and turned in his bed. It didn't feel quite so comfy and cosy any more.

"Mouse!" Bear whispered, just in case Mouse was awake too. But Mouse didn't reply, so Bear whispered again, a bit louder. "Mouse! MOUSE! I can't sleep. It's too hot in this cave. Could you open your window?"

Mouse woke up – just a little bit – and blearily he opened his window. "Is that better, Bear?" he asked, falling back into bed.

"That's perfect, thank you, Mouse," said Bear, much happier, as a gentle breeze floated through the room.

"Marvellous. Night-night, Bear," said Mouse, and with a small sigh he fell back asleep. *Psssh-pssh-pssh.*

Bear couldn't believe it. Mouse was asleep again! Already! How was that possible, when Bear was still awake on his own?

"Pah," Bear sighed. The breeze was cool, and it was lovely, but he was not even a tiny bit asleep and it was very unfair.

"Mouse!" he called (not even bothering to whisper this time).

"MOUSE! Wake up! I can't sleep. Your night-light is too bright and it's keeping me awake!"

"Hm?" said Mouse, half awake. "Sorry, Bear," and he leaned over and turned off the night-light. *Click!* Then Mouse settled back into his small, comfy bed, turned over once . . . and fell fast asleep. *Psssh-pssh-pssh.*

"Bah!" tutted Bear. Mouse hadn't even woken up! Bear was sure of it. How did he do it? How dare he? Surely Mouse should realise that his friend needed company, awake alone in the dark. The very dark dark.

Without Mouse's night-light the room was black and there were no twinkly stars dancing over the ceiling to look at. Bear lay in the very dark, feeling very, very cross.

Psssh-pssh-pssh.

Sigh. Harumph.

What was a bear to do?

Psssh-pssh-pssh. Psssh-pssh-pssh.

That was it! Bear had had enough.

"MOUSE!" shouted Bear. "STOP SNORING! You're keeping me awake and it's VERY selfish!"

At last Mouse was properly awake. But Mouse was also properly cross. "I wasn't snoring!" he snapped. "And if I'm so very selfish then I'm going outside to sleep in the garden where I WON'T ANNOY ANYONE!" And with that Mouse picked up his blanket and stomped outside. *Slam!* went the door, and the cave fell silent.

Bear lay in his bed feeling rather alone. The cave was very, very dark and very, very quiet. Too quiet. And Bear didn't just feel alone, he felt sad and ever so mean. Why had he been so horrible to his friend Mouse? Mouse hadn't done anything wrong.

"Oh dear," sighed Bear. "Oh bother." What if Mouse was cold in the garden? What if he was scared of the dark, out in the big outdoors all alone?

Bear leapt out of his bed in a fluster. "Mouse!" he cried, rushing out into the garden with his blanket. "Mouse! I'm so sorry. I didn't mean to be horrible. It wasn't you keeping me awake. I don't want you to be alone out in the dark. I'll keep you company."

Mouse turned to Bear and smiled his gentle smile. "Oh, Bear, that's OK. I know you didn't mean it. And it's rather fun camping in the garden, you know." And Mouse gave Bear a big goodnight hug, snuggled up in his cosy blanket, and fell fast asleep.

Bear looked round the peaceful garden and smiled. The bushes and trees were magical in the moonlight. Ever-so-quietly Bear put his blanket next to the sleeping Mouse, then curled up on the soft grass. It was a beautiful night. The breeze drifted softly over them, and high above the stars twinkled brightly. The sound of crickets made a gentle lullaby and, best of all, the most comforting and perfect sound to fall asleep to, Bear could hear the quiet *psssh-pssh-pssh* of his best friend Mouse.

"Night-night, Mouse," whispered Bear softly. And he turned over, gave a big sigh, and fell fast asleep.

Bedtime For Little Bunny

Written by Josephine Collins

Illustrated by Jo Parry

Bedtime For Little Bunny

On Buttercup Hill, as the sun was setting, the rabbits were getting ready for bed. Warm in their burrow, sleepy baby bunnies were having their evening wash.

"Lickety-lick and in you go!" Mama Rabbit sang, as she scooped them up, one by one, to wash their ears and pop them into bed.

But one little bunny was still full of bounce. "I do not like ear washes," he grumbled, "and I do not like bedtime all squished up in this hole!" And with that, he wriggled away and hoppity-skipped out of the burrow.

"I'll have more fun at Owley's," Little Bunny decided, bouncing down the hill. At the owls' tree, Little Bunny was just in time to join Owley for a snack.

"Hello!" cried Owley, giving his friend a big hug. "Look what I've got – honey toast! Do you want some?"

"Yummy! Yes, please!" said Little Bunny.

"Shouldn't you be at home?" smiled Mama Owl. "The moon is out which means it's sleepy-time for rabbits!"

"Not for me! I'm not sleepy yet," Little Bunny said.

In the bright
moonlight, Little
Bunny and Owley
munched their toast, and gazed
up at the stars. But the wind was
whistling through the leaves of Owley's
tree and soon Little Bunny felt chilly.
Brrr! This is not like my cosy, dark burrow, he
thought to himself, shivering. *Perhaps I'll
go and visit Hoglet. His house is always nice
and warm.*

"I have to go, Owley," said Little Bunny.
"Night night, and thank you for the toast!"

As Little Bunny reached the hedgehogs' nest, he could see Hoglet and his brothers and sisters tumbling down a mossy bank.

"Come and join us, Little Bunny!" said Hoglet. "We're having a race!"

"That sounds fun!" giggled Little Bunny, and he curled up into a ball and roly-polied down the slope.

"Whoops! I'm not as fast as you!" laughed Little Bunny, landing with a bump.

"You're out very late!" said Hoglet. "Isn't it your bedtime now?"

"Not just yet! I can stay a bit longer," said Little Bunny.

So the friends huddled up in the hedgehogs' cosy nest and made leaf pictures together. But Little Bunny kept wriggling, and fidgeting. Whichever way he sat he got prickled by one of the hedgehogs!

It may be warm, but it's not soft and comfy here like my burrow! he thought to himself. *Perhaps I'll visit Little Beaver. Her home always seems snug.* "I have to go, Hoglet!" he called. "Let's play again soon!"

Little Bunny hoppity-skipped along the riverbank to the beavers' lodge, where Mama Beaver was singing a song. "Just like my mummy does at bedtime!" Little Bunny laughed.

"Hello, Little Bunny!" said Little Beaver who was jumping and spinning around. "Do you want to dance with me?" she asked.

"Yes, please!" said Little Bunny. And they both twirled and skipped together.

"Aren't you sleepy?" asked Mama Beaver, when the song was finished. "We're used to being up at night, but it's late for little rabbits to be awake!"

"I'm not sleepy yet . . ." yawned Little Bunny. "I can stay up a bit longer." So Little Bunny and Little Beaver played a game of hide-and-seek.

But before long, Little Bunny's paws were wet and his whiskers were muddy from playing in the beavers' watery home.

This is no place for a bunny like me, he thought to himself. *I think I need to find somewhere dry and comfy!*

"It's time for me to go, Little Beaver," Little Bunny called out. "Thank you for having me! See you soon!"

"Who do I know who has a warm, dry, cosy home?" he wondered aloud, as he slowly hopped along. "Why, Mousey, of course!"

At Mousey's hedge, Little Bunny could hear Mama Mouse reading a story.

"I know this one!" cried Little Bunny. "It's my favourite!"

"You can come inside and listen if you like," said Mama Mouse.

"Yes, please!" said Little Bunny, peeping into the mousehole.

"I'll help you in!" squeaked Mousey, giving Little Bunny's ears a tug, but he couldn't squeeze through.

"I'll try coming in backwards," said Little Bunny. So Mousey gave Little Bunny's tail a tug. But try as he might, Little Bunny could not fit in the mouses' tiny home!

"It's no good," he puffed, poking his head back into the hole. "I'll just have to listen like this."

And so, with Mousey snuggled up next to his whiskers, the two friends enjoyed a lovely story. But by the end, Little Bunny's bottom was freezing!

This is not at all like my bedtime story cuddled up with Mummy . . . Little Bunny thought, sadly. And suddenly he longed to be back in his cosy burrow!

"Night night, Mousey," he said wearily. "Now it's time for me to go home." Mama Mouse waved him goodbye, and watched as he hopped sleepily back up the hill.

Back in the burrow, squished up cosily, Little Bunny snuggled with all the other bunnies for a big, bedtime cuddle. "What an adventure I've had," he whispered, "but there's nothing better than being at home!"

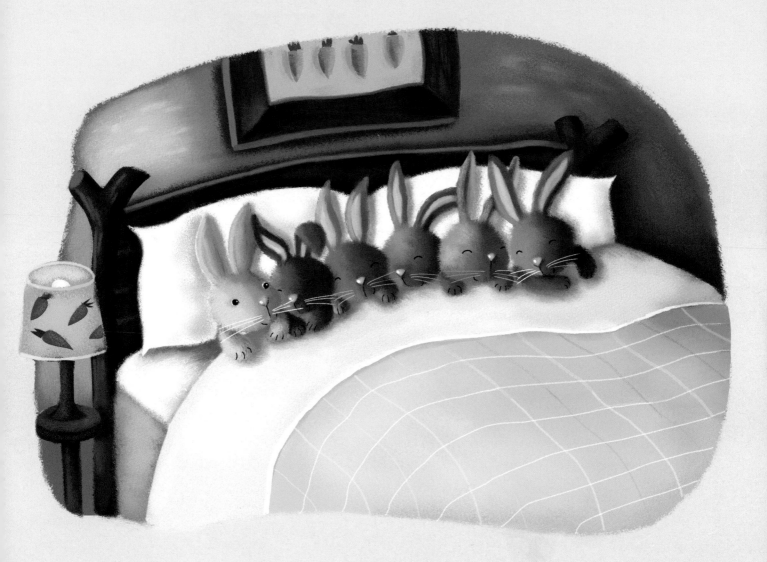

Jack And The Monster

Written by Stephanie Stansbie

Illustrated by Emi Ordás

Jack And The Monster

"RARGH! Ready or not, here I come!" yelled Jack, taking his hands from his eyes and stomping round the bedroom. He searched the wardrobe and the toy box, and was just about to look behind the door when his mum called up the stairs.

"Bedtime!"

"But I'm playing monster hide-and-seek," cried Jack. "And it's my turn to find the monster!"

"You can play monsters tomorrow," his mum said. "Right now it's time for bed."

"But I really, really can't go to bed," Jack explained, leaning over the banister. "The monster won't know where I've gone – he'll be hiding all night!"

"OK," Mum smiled. "You've got five minutes to find the monster, and then it's time to brush your teeth."

When Jack had finished his game, Mum herded him into the bathroom.

"I can't find my toothbrush," said Jack. "I think the monster's eaten it!"

"The rascal!" said Mum. "He'd better give it back quick, or there'll be no time for a story."

"Oh, it's down here, behind the radiator," said Jack, pulling out a rather fluffy-looking toothbrush. "The monster must've hidden it because he doesn't want me to go to bed."

Jack brushed his teeth, then got into his pyjamas – very slowly. "I don't think I can go to sleep yet, Mum," he said. "I asked the monster, and he says he's not tired AT ALL."

"Well, maybe a story will help make him sleepy," Mum replied. "Have you chosen one?"

Jack nodded and pulled an enormous, heavy book from the shelf: *Monstrously Massive Monster Stories.* "The monster wants you to read this."

"I'm not reading all of that!" Mum said.

"No, no, no," said Jack. "Eight stories is fine."

"Three," Mum laughed.

"Nine," replied Jack.

So Jack snuggled up in bed and Mum read him four monster stories.

Then she turned out the light. "Sleep tight," she whispered. "Mind the monsters don't bite."

"Monsters don't really bite," said Jack. "That's just a silly saying."

"You're right," said Mum. "Now go to sleep."

But she hadn't been downstairs long before Jack called out, "Muuuuum! The monster needs a drink!"

So Mum trudged back up with a glass of water.

"Thanks, Mum! The monster's very thirsty," Jack explained. "He's been busy doing monstering all day."

"Oh has he now?" said Mum. "Well you tell the monster that once he's drunk his water it'll be time to settle down and GO TO SLEEP!"

"Don't worry," said Jack, "We will, I promise." And he snuggled back under his duvet.

For a few minutes all was quiet and Mum breathed a sigh of relief.
But it wasn't long before Jack called, "Mu-um! The monster needs a blanket!
He says he's cold."

Next the monster needed another pillow.

Then a biscuit.

"Monstering makes you very hungry, you know!" said Jack.

Jack's mum had had enough. "It's getting really late now, and if you're not asleep very soon I'll turn into Angry Monster Mummy." And she turned off the light once more.

"I know I'm meant to be going to sleep Mum," said Jack in a hushed voice, "but the monster wants to tell you something!"

Jack's mum sighed and turned the light back on. "Where is this monster then?" she asked.

"Under the bed of course!" said Jack, sitting up against his pillows. "But he's shy. So I'll tell you instead."

"Quickly then," said Mum.

"The thing is," Jack whispered, "the monster is actually a little bit scared. That's why he doesn't want to go to sleep. It's very dark under the bed, and he's afraid of the dark."

"Oh I see!" said Mum. "Is that what this has all been about?"

Jack nodded, and Mum smiled. "Silly monster should've told me before," she said. "He probably just needs a cuddle."

"Ooh yes!" said Jack. "That'll make him feel better."

So Mum went to fetch Jack's old battered bear, and his night-light from when he was a baby. Carefully she popped them under the bed.

"I'll just leave these here – in case you need them too," she said.

"Oh, I don't need them," said Jack. "I'm a big boy!"

Mum sang Jack a lovely lullaby. Then she gave him a great big cuddle.

"Mum," whispered Jack. "Me and the monster love you a whole lot. We think you are the very bestest mum in the whole world."

Mum smiled and kissed him on the nose. Then Jack did a gigantic yawn, rolled over and went to sleep.

And the monster? The monster did exactly the same . . .

A Lullaby
For Baby Blue

Written by Sarah Powell

Illustrated by Tim Budgen

A Lullaby For Baby Blue

Every night, just before bedtime, Mama Whale would sing a song for Baby Blue. Mama's beautiful voice would drift and soar through the twinkling ocean and Baby Blue would fall fast asleep, bobbing gently beside her.

But one night, Blue could not sleep. In the morning, she was going on a long journey south with her family. It was going to be a very big adventure.

"Mama," asked Blue, "what happens if I lose you along the way?"

"Don't worry, Blue, your Papa and I will look after you. And remember, if you get lost, just sing out and we will find you."

But Blue knew she could not sing. She had tried to join in with her parents' beautiful songs, but her voice just wouldn't come out right.

Her mama always told her that she would be able to sing when she needed to, but Blue wasn't sure. All Blue could think about was what would happen if she did get lost. How would her mama and papa find her? She cuddled close to Mama and tried to sleep, but all too soon it was morning.

"Wakey, wakey, everyone!" cried Papa. "Are you ready for our big adventure?"

"I think so," yawned Blue, stretching out her flippers. But she didn't feel ready.

"1-2-3, it's swim time! Let's go!" sang Papa, swooshing his tail. Blue had never seen him so excited.

Blue stuck close to her parents, and as they swam southwards Mama and Papa sang together. Gradually the ocean changed from icy dark to warm, crystal blue and all around them the sea sparkled with brightly coloured creatures.

"Wow!" exclaimed Blue. "What's that? It's so beautiful!"

"That's a coral reef," explained Mama. "Would you like to take a look?" They swam over to the reef, where they met a family of seahorses.

"My name is Bobbin," said the littlest seahorse. "Who are you?"

"I'm Blue," exclaimed Blue, excitedly. "Nice to meet you! Would you like to swim with us?"

So off they went. Before long they passed a shipwreck, where they met a lobster named Claude, who had the biggest claws Blue had ever seen.

"Will you swim with us, too?" giggled Blue. So Claude swam with them, clapping along to the whales' songs, as the seahorses sang the chorus. Blue laughed aloud with joy. She was starting to enjoy her adventure very much indeed.

The further they swam the more wonderful creatures they met. But as they travelled, Blue noticed how each one was able to join their own voice to the whales' singing in a magical ocean song, and she felt rather left out.

"Why am I the only one without a voice?" wondered Blue, sadly.

Suddenly, a huge shoal of colourful fish zoomed by. They weren't singing. The fish were *shouting* as they flew past Blue and her parents, zipping about in all directions.

"Out of the way!" cried one. "Coming through!"

"Must hurry!" exclaimed another. "Storm's coming!"

"I'm scared!" wailed Blue.

"Just stick with us," called Papa, "and remember to sing out if you get lost!"

At first, Blue swam safely between Mama and Papa, but when the storm came the waters began to roll her left and right, and up and down. She pushed forward with her tiny tail and flippers, but the current was too strong.

"Let's swim nearer the bottom of the ocean," cried Papa. "It should be calmer down there."

But the storm had stirred up the sea bed, and seaweed and sand were whirling around everywhere.

"I can't see you," called Baby Blue, as the ocean swirled like mist all around her. "Mama? Papa?" Blue cried, but her voice wasn't loud enough for them to hear.

Feeling dizzy and tired she sank to the ocean floor alone. As the storm spun around her, Blue closed her eyes and waited for it to pass. When at last the waters cleared, she discovered that she was back at the reef but her parents were nowhere to be seen. Blue began to cry.

"Are you all right?" said a friendly voice. It was Bobbin, and Claude too. "What a storm! We had to hide in a coral cave."

"Achoo!" sneezed Claude, who had sand up his nose. "Do you know where your parents are?"

Blue shook her head sadly. "And I'll never find them now because I can't sing!" she sobbed.

Claude and Bobbin comforted Blue until she could cry no more, then they swam with her up to the ocean's surface. Blue poked her head above the waves, and saw a beautiful sunset shimmering across the now-calm sea. She could see a long way in every direction, but there was no sign of Mama or Papa.

Just then, through her sadness, Blue remembered her mama's voice. *You'll be able to sing when you need to, my Baby Blue.* Her mama had been so sure. Blue had to give it one more try. She took a deep breath – and out came one long, clear note.

"You can do it, Blue!" cried Bobbin and Claude, swimming round her. "Try again!"

With her friends' encouragement, Blue started to sing. Her voice was quiet at first, but it soon became stronger and louder, and it was beautiful. She was really singing!

Suddenly, glorious whale song echoed all around them. It was Mama! And there were more voices, too. The ocean was filled with a choir of whales singing back to her, happy that the storm was over.

"Oh Baby Blue, we found you!" cried Mama and Papa, rushing towards her.

"I thought I had lost you," said Blue, "but my friends found me and then I found my voice!"

"You've been very brave, Blue," said Papa, cuddling her.

For the rest of the day, Blue played with her new friends, laughing, swimming and best of all . . . singing! When it was time to sleep, Mama began to sing a new song.

"1-2-3, it's sleepy time for me," yawned Papa.

"But I'm not tired at all," yawned Blue.

"Are you sure about that?" giggled Mama.

"I'm very sure," said Blue. "I could sing all day and all night." Then, with one eye closing, she asked Mama, "What's that song you're singing?"

"It's a special bedtime lullaby for you, my brave Baby Blue," said Mama softly.

"I'll sing along, too," mumbled Blue, but she was already falling asleep, dreaming of rainbow reefs, new friends and a journey she would never forget.

Baby Bertie's Noisy Night

Written by Lucy M. George

Illustrated by Sarah Jennings

Baby Bertie's Noisy Night

Baby Bertie was a very quiet baby. He didn't cry all the time like other babies; in fact, hardly anything seemed to bother him. "Is he always this peaceful?" people often asked.

All day long he snoozed in his little basket, while his family busily, and rather noisily, went about their business around him. Bertie didn't have a care in the world.

Bertie's mummy liked to sing. "TRA LA LAA LA LAA!" she warbled at the top of her voice, right next to Bertie. She sang so loudly even the neighbours could hear. RAT-A-TAT-TAT, they knocked on the wall.

"PLEASE KEEP IT DOWN!" they shouted. But Baby Bertie didn't cry.

His daddy did the washing up, clattering the pots and pans.

CRASH BANG CLATTER! He banged them so loudly even the neighbours could hear. RAT-A-TAT-TAT, they knocked on the wall.

"PLEASE KEEP IT DOWN!" they shouted. But Baby Bertie didn't cry.

His sister, Celia, who was noisier than Mummy and Daddy put together, played her favourite game which mostly involved screaming loudly, "AHH, OOH, AHH, RAAAAR!!!" She screamed so loudly even the neighbours could hear. RAT-A-TAT-TAT, they banged on the wall.

"PLEASE DO KEEP IT DOWN!" they shouted. But still Bertie didn't cry.

Bertie's Granny and Granddad rang the bell, RIIING! His Auntie and Uncle knocked on the door, BANG BANG! They all chinked their tea cups, they talked and laughed loudly.

"What a beautiful baby! He's so quiet!" Auntie shrieked.

"Does he ever cry?!" Uncle boomed. They even passed him around the room, but Baby Bertie didn't cry once.

Just when you'd think the house couldn't get any louder, Bertie's little cousins came to visit. They emptied a tub of bricks on the floor, played the piano, banged the drums, and even played Dinosaurs and Lions, where everyone roared very loudly. They roared so loudly the neighbours roared back.

"ARGHHHHHHHHH!" their voices came through the wall. "PLEASE WILL YOU KEEP IT DOWN IN THERE!" they shouted. But Bertie didn't cry. In fact, he giggled.

After a long day of singing, banging pots and screaming, at last it was bedtime for Bertie's family. They brushed their teeth and put their pyjamas on. Celia gave Bertie a kiss and snuggled down to sleep. Mummy gave Bertie a kiss and climbed into bed. Daddy gave Bertie a kiss and whispered, "Night night, Bertie," then turned out the light. The house fell silent at last.

And just at that moment, Bertie's mouth opened and he started to cry. "WAAAAAAAAAAAAH!" he yelled.

"I'll go," said Mummy, sleepily. Mummy went into Bertie's room and picked him up. "Hush hush, Bertie," she whispered. "Would you like some milk?" She tried feeding him, but Bertie wasn't hungry. She tried singing him a gentle lullaby, but Bertie didn't like it. She tried rocking him.

"WAAA!" Bertie cried.

Bertie was making so much noise that Daddy woke up. He went into Bertie's room. "Let me try," whispered Daddy, taking his little boy in his arms.

Daddy gave Bertie a cuddle. "Hush hush, Bertie," he whispered. "Do you need a clean nappy?" He checked Bertie's nappy, but it wasn't dirty. He patted his bottom, but Bertie didn't like it. He tried stroking his head.

"WAAAH!" Bertie cried.

Bertie was making so much noise that Celia woke up. "Let me try," whispered his sister, taking her little brother in her arms.

Celia gave Bertie a cuddle. "Hush hush, Bertie," she whispered. "Would you like me to read to you?" She quietly read him a story, but Bertie didn't want a story. She tried gently jiggling him, but Bertie didn't like it. She tried rubbing his tummy.

"WAAAAAAAAAAAAH!" Bertie cried, louder than ever.

Soon, the neighbours were awake. RAT-A-TAT-TAT, they knocked on the wall. "WILL YOU PLEASE PLEASE PLEASE KEEP IT DOWN!" they shouted.

"WAAAAAH!" Bertie cried.

"SORRY!" shouted Mummy through the wall. "BERTIE WON'T GO TO SLEEP!"

"SORRY!" shouted Daddy, "WE'RE TRYING EVERYTHING WE CAN THINK OF!"

"SORRY!" shouted Celia, and then she shouted, "RAAAAR!" because everyone was shouting already and she really liked making noise.

And guess what? Bertie stopped crying! All the banging and all the shouting had stopped Bertie wailing. And his eyes were starting to close . . .

"It's working!" said Mummy.

"Keep roaring, Celia!" said Daddy.

"WHAT?" shouted the neighbours through the wall.

"NOT YOU!" shouted Celia. And then she leaned in close to her little brother and not too loudly, but just loudly enough, she went, "RAAAAR!"

And Bertie fell fast asleep.

The Surprise Sleepover

Written by Juliet Groom

Illustrated by Lucy Fleming

The Surprise Sleepover

It was nearly bedtime in number 15 Broad Street and Cecily Long was just running the bath when the doorbell rang loudly. DING DONG!

She peeped through the banister as Mummy opened the door. There on the step was a small green crocodile with a large overnight bag.

"I've come for the sleepover!" announced the crocodile happily, and in he toddled.

Cecily rushed down the stairs two at a time. A crocodile? Here for a sleepover? Fantastic!

Mummy was reading a letter the crocodile had passed to her.

DEAR HORACE,
PLEASE come to a
FABULOUS sleep over at
number 15. Tonight at 7pm.
Bring your armbands!

Lots of Love, the Hippos

"Oh dear!" said Mummy to Daddy. "I think they meant number 15 River Street, not Broad Street. He'll have to go!"

"But it's too late to send a little crocodile out on his own now!" cried Cecily. "He'll have to stay with me. I promise we'll be good! Pleeceease!"

Mummy looked at Daddy and then at Horace the crocodile. Horace gave a polite, toothy smile. And Cecily hopped from foot to foot and wished the biggest wish of her life. Pleeeeeease let him stay!

"OK," Mummy smiled. "He can stay, just for tonight. But do try not to make too much noise, or mess." (Cecily was very good at adventures, but adventures were sometimes rather noisy. And very messy.)

"Hooray!" shouted Cecily. "He can have the bottom bunk! Come on, Horace!"

"Yippee!" said Horace, and they rushed upstairs two at a time.

"Time for our bath, Horace!" ordered Cecily. She put in lots of bubbles and LOTS of toys to play with. It was such fun. Horace was the splashiest bath companion ever. He wore hilarious armbands and Mummy's spotty bath hat.

He sang loudly and giggled and splashed and Cecily sang loudly and giggled and splashed and soon there was water and bubbles everywhere.

"Ce-cily!" shouted Daddy up the stairs. "Out of the bath and ready for bed!"

"Ooops!" gasped Cecily, looking at the mess. But as she hopped out to dry the bathroom she heard a strange, slightly suspicious, crunching sound.

"Yummy yummy." Burp. "Thank you," said Horace.

"The bath hat! My boat! Oh noooo! GIVE ME BACK THAT DUCK!" shouted Cecily, hurriedly rescuing her favourite duck before Horace could eat it.

Cecily thought anxiously of all the toys in her bedroom that Horace might eat. "Maybe we should have a snack," she said as she handed him a stripy towel.

"Oooh yummy! Yes, please," said Horace politely and he toddled down to the kitchen after Cecily.

Daddy made Cecily's MOST favourite snack – chocolate chip biscuits and hot, frothy milk.

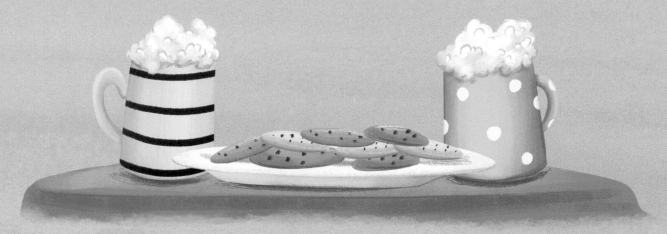

"Yummy!" grinned Horace. Before Cecily could blink the heap of biscuits was gone. There was only one left for Cecily!

"My," said Daddy, "Horace is very hungry for such a small crocodile, isn't he?"

"Yes, please, thank you," said Horace politely.

So Daddy made toast, and cereal, and the BIGGEST midnight feast plate of pancakes Cecily had ever seen, and Horace ate it all. Every bit. He even ate the plate and the salt and pepper pots!

"Stop, Horace!" shouted Cecily, whisking the milk jug out of Horace's reach.

"Yummy yummy." Atchoo! "Sorry, thank you," grinned Horace.

He snuggled up to Cecily and she laughed. "Are you full at last? Would you like a cuddle?"

But as Horace leaned over he just gobbled up the last of Cecily's biscuit! Gulp. "Yummy!" Burp. "Thank you!"

Cecily was cross. "That's not fair!" she shouted. There were no biscuits left and no cereal for breakfast and this was NOT how a sleepover should work. But she looked at Horace's wobbly, apologetic smile and thought quietly. Maybe crocodiles didn't learn about sharing until they were older. Maybe they'd be better at bedtime stories.

"Thank you for supper, Daddy," she said, and together Cecily and Horace stomped upstairs to brush their teeth.

"Did you bring a toothbrush?" Cecily asked Horace. Horace shook his head. "Would you like to borrow one?" asked Cecily. Horace nodded. So Cecily told him VERY strictly that he was NOT to eat it.

And Horace was very very good. He brushed his teeth till they were sparkling. And then he showed Cecily how to draw toothpaste pictures on the mirror and it was brilliant. She'd never done that at a sleepover before!

In her bedroom Horace squeezed himself into the bottom bunk with his cuddly sock monkey. Cecily squeezed in next to him and Mummy read them FIVE bedtime stories. Horace and Cecily made the animal noises and sang pirate songs and it was the loudest, bounciest, best story time ever!

At last Horace yawned a big toothy yawn and Mummy kissed them both goodnight. Cecily climbed up to her top bunk.

Cecily snuggled down. She was a bit cramped as she had all of her toys with her, just in case Horace got peckish in the night, but that was OK. It had been the best sleepover ever.

"Night-night, Horace," she said.

"Yummy, night-night, thank you," said Horace, and he fell fast asleep.

As Cecily drifted off to sleep she thought about the letter from the Hippos and wondered if they'd had a fun sleepover too. Tomorrow she would write back to them. Mummy and Daddy wouldn't mind if a couple of hippos came for a sleepover one night, she was sure!

Jess's Farm

Written by Josephine Collins

Illustrated by Kim Barnes

Jess's Farm

Jess thought her farm was the most perfect place to live in the world. It was just a small farm with a few cows, and sheep, a horse and some chickens. Jess loved playing in the farmyard, she loved the rolling green hills at the back of the farmhouse, and the little river at the bottom of the fields. And most of all Jess loved the animals.

Whenever Jess had the chance she would help out in the farmyard. Every morning, she would go with her mum to feed the animals. She couldn't possibly leave for school without saying good morning to each of her friends.

"Hello, Daisy!" she would call out to the oldest milk cow.

"Good morning! And how are you today?" she would say to the chickens. And as she gave them all a stroke or a pat, she felt sure that, in their own special way, they said hello back to her.

After school, Jess would help to groom their horse, Molly, or milk the cows – there was always so much to do! Whatever task Dad had given her, Jess would sing to the animals as she worked. And if ever the animals were upset, Jess would calm them with a song.

"I don't know how you do it, Jess," Dad said, as they walked together back up to the farmhouse one evening. "You could get those animals to do anything with that beautiful voice of yours!"

Jess smiled and said, "They're my friends. I understand them, and they understand me."

That spring, there were two new arrivals on the farm. Up at the farmhouse, Jess's new baby brother Jack was born, and in the farmyard there was a new baby lamb, who Jess named Meg. Jess was so excited, she could hardly wait to get home from school each day to see them both.

"I'm not sure who I love the most!" Jess giggled, as she tickled her baby brother's tummy and gave him kisses on his tiny toes to make him smile. "You're the cutest baby brother ever, Jack! But I do love my cuddles with Meg, too!"

But very soon, Jess began to see changes around her little farm. Jess's mum and dad were tired all the time, and there wasn't as much time for playing or singing together. Baby Jack wasn't sleeping, and at night he just cried and cried. Jess and Mum and Dad tried singing different lullabies to Jack to help him sleep, but none of them worked. Jess was worried, and the animals seemed upset too. If only Jack would stop crying! She wished things would just go back to normal.

One evening when she was feeling particularly glum, she decided to visit Meg to cheer herself up. As she headed along the track to the farmyard, she heard a faint sound carried on the breeze. Jess was sure she could hear Molly's gentle neighs, and the cows softly mooing.

"Whatever can be happening?" she wondered. Then she heard the sheep baaing and the chickens cluck clucking – and all of these familiar sounds were blending together to make the most beautiful music Jess had ever heard. The animals were singing together the songs that Jess had taught them. It was amazing! Jess raced down into the yard, and there, in amongst all the animals, was Meg sleeping soundly.

Suddenly, Jess knew what she needed to do. "This wonderful music is sure to help baby Jack sleep too!" she gasped. "Oh, you clever animals! Thank you!" Jess cried, as she hugged all of her friends.

With Meg fast asleep in her arms, Jess led the animals all the way to the farmhouse, where they could hear Jack crying inside. "If we sing together," said Jess, "baby Jack is sure to be soothed to sleep!" So the animals and Jess sang, and soon the whole farm was filled with the sounds of happy, lilting music.

Before long the crying stopped, and Jess's mum and dad came out to watch in wonder.

"Thank you, Jess. Your music has helped baby Jack fall asleep," Dad whispered, giving Jess a big hug.

That night, everyone slept soundly, and in the morning Jess went to visit the animals to say thank you.

After that, things got much better on the farm. Jess and the animals would often sing their special song to help Jack sleep. And as he grew bigger, Jess began teaching Jack how to sing too!

Jess and Jack loved playing together in the farmyard, or in the rolling green hills at the back of the farmhouse, or by the little river at the bottom of the fields. But most of all they both loved their friends the animals.

The Boy With The Magic Pyjamas

Written by Stephanie Stansbie

Illustrated by Ian Cunliffe

The Boy With The Magic Pyjamas

Stan's Uncle Eric was an explorer. He went all over the world discovering things, and he always brought Stan something strange and wonderful from his adventures.

Stan couldn't wait to be an explorer too. Whenever his uncle came to stay, Stan would beg: "I want to come with you!"

But Uncle Eric would just laugh and say, "Not today, Stan."

Until one day . . . Stan was getting ready for bed when he heard his uncle's booming voice. He raced downstairs and jumped into his arms.

"Slow down, young man!" laughed Uncle Eric.

"What have you got? What have you got?" Stan cried.

Uncle Eric smiled and reached into his battered old rucksack. "I've got a very special present for you," he said as he handed Stan something small and crumpled.

"Oh," said Stan. It didn't look very exciting! "What is it?"

"Pyjamas!" Uncle Eric said.

"Pyjamas?" mumbled Stan, disappointed. "They don't look very special."

"That's because you're not looking hard enough," whispered Eric, with a twinkle.

"Thanks," said Stan quietly, and kissed his uncle on the cheek. Then he went slowly up the stairs.

"I'm not putting them on," he grumbled to himself. "They're the rubbishest present ever." But then he thought about what Uncle Eric had said. Stan looked a bit closer at the pyjamas and saw that they were covered in pictures. One was a boy on a magic carpet, one was a rocket, another a pirate ship.

"Maybe I will wear them – just for a bit," he decided. Stan clambered into bed. The pyjamas were warm and soft. Soon he started to feel sleepy . . .

Suddenly he heard a whooshing sound. A warm wind was blowing against his cheek and it felt like he was moving really fast. Stan sat up and looked around. The ground was far below him. He was flying on a magic carpet!

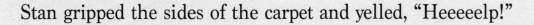

Stan gripped the sides of the carpet and yelled, "Heeeeelp!"

"Don't worry," said a voice. "You'll get used to it in a minute." It was Uncle Eric! He was whizzing along beside him on a carpet of his own.

"What's happening?" squealed Stan.

"We're exploring!" shouted Uncle Eric.

Stan took a deep breath and peered over the side. Beneath him were waves of sand. Far in the distance, a golden temple was lit up against the moon.

"Woaaah!" cried Stan as the two magic carpets swooped down towards the ground.

"Pull up!" yelled Uncle Eric.

But it was too late – Stan landed head first in a huge dune. SPLAT!

"Nice landing!" chuckled Eric, pulling Stan out by his feet.

"Ouch!" squealed Stan. "There's something hard in the sand!"

Uncle Eric dug down and pulled out a grubby bottle with a cork stopper pushed into the end. The glass was cracked where Stan had crashed into it. All of a sudden, there came a hissing sound and a cloud of green gas billowed out through the crack.

"Now you've done it!" whispered
Uncle Eric.

The gas started to thicken and change
shape, until there was an enormous
green man floating above them.

"I am the genie of the bottle!" thundered
the green man, looking straight at Stan.

"You have set me free. I grant you three wishes."

Stan looked at Uncle Eric, his eyes wide.

"Can I really wish for anything at all?" he asked.

"Of course!" smiled Uncle Eric. "But choose carefully."

Stan thought hard. But his tummy was rumbling and
he couldn't concentrate.

"I wish we had something to eat!" he blurted out.

Instantly, a huge feast was laid out before them.

There was smoked meat, sumptuous fruit and sweet
treats dusted with
sugar.

"Oops!" said Stan. "I didn't mean to wish that." But the food was so delicious that they both tucked in, and soon they forgot all about the genie floating above them.

"That was amazing!" sighed Stan, brushing the sugar from his lips. "But I wish we had something to drink." Suddenly a silver flagon of lemonade appeared in front of him. "Oh no!" squealed Stan. "I wasted another wish!"

"You have only one left," boomed the genie. "Think carefully!"

"I wish," said Stan slowly, "I wish I could go with Uncle Eric on all his adventures!"

"Your wish is my command!" said the genie. "Just look hard enough, and you can have all the adventures you like." With that, the genie disappeared in a cloud of smoke.

Stan blinked and rubbed his eyes. When he opened them again, he was back home in his own bed.

"That was incredible," he whispered. But Stan was puzzled. He couldn't figure out what the genie had meant. Look hard enough at what?

He was still thinking about it, when at last he fell asleep.

The next morning, Stan ran straight downstairs and found his uncle packing to go.

"Did we really fly on magic carpets last night?" asked Stan.

But Uncle Eric just smiled. Then he gave him a great big hug.

"Take care, Stan. I'll see you soon."

When he had gone, Stan sat on the sofa feeling glum. He looked down at his pyjamas. Then he blinked and looked again. "That's me!" he gasped.

The picture of the boy on the magic carpet – it was Stan! Stan looked closer. He was in all of the pictures! There he was in the rocket – and there in the pirate ship! That's what the genie had meant, the pyjamas were magic. Stan could use them to go with Uncle Eric on all his adventures!

"Wow!" Stan whispered. "I wonder where we'll go exploring tonight . . ."

The Midnight Feast

Written by Becky Davies

Illustrated by Emi Ordás

The Midnight Feast

"Why do you always have to be so annoying?" snapped Tom at his little sister, Katie.

Katie stopped humming and looked up at him. Then she went back to spreading jam on her fourth piece of toast.

"I wish you two would learn to get along," sighed Mum. "Why don't you ever play together?"

Tom frowned at Katie across the breakfast table. It wasn't *his* fault that she was so annoying. She was always doing silly things, and pestering him to play. But he didn't want to play with her. She was just a baby – and worse still, a *girl*.

"Do you want to know a top-secret secret?" Katie whispered loudly to her brother when Mum's back was turned.

"No," said Tom. "I'm going to play football with Billy. It's probably a rubbish secret anyway." He was just about to leave, when he saw her slip all four pieces of jammy toast into her pockets.

Katie caught him looking, and pressed a finger to her lips.

Tom shook his head. *Just some silly baby game,* he decided. Then he raced up to his room to change into his football kit.

Mum called up the stairs a moment later. "Billy's mum just rang, Tom – poor Billy's sick and can't play today after all."

"Ooh, maybe you'd like to join in with my top-secret secret now?" said Katie. Tom hadn't noticed her until then. She was rummaging through the laundry basket, pulling out all the dirty socks. How strange!

"No thank you," Tom replied, trying to sound important. "I'm very busy today." And he hurried off to watch some television. But Tom couldn't concentrate. He kept seeing Katie skipping past the doorway with handfuls of dandelions and daisies, singing happily to herself. What *was* she up to?

At lunchtime, Tom counted *fifteen* carrot sticks being added to Katie's already bulging pockets. He hated to admit it, but he *really* wanted to know what she was doing. By mid-afternoon Tom could bear it no longer.

"What's this super special top-secret secret then?" he demanded.

"You have to pinky promise not to tell," said Katie solemnly, offering her hand up to her big brother.

"Okay," sighed Tom, linking fingers. "I promise."

"I'm having a tea party tonight!" cried Katie gleefully.

Tom groaned. "A tea party? I knew it was a rubbish secret!"

"It's going to be so much fun," continued Katie. "All of my toys are coming! And you can come too if you like."

"Ha!" laughed Tom, "I'm far too grown up for a toys' tea party thank you very much." And he marched off, delighted that he'd found out Katie's silly secret.

All afternoon Tom played by himself, but he had to admit that it wasn't much fun. He kicked his ball against a wall, grumpily. "I know," he thought, "I'll eat my birthday chocolate. Katie's too busy organising her stupid tea party to pester me for some. I'll be able to have it all to myself." He fetched the bar and unwrapped it carefully. But after only one square he wrapped it back up. Somehow it didn't taste so good by himself.

Just then Katie skipped past in her pyjamas. She seemed to be having a lot of fun without him.

Tom bit his lip. Maybe he'd been mean to her earlier . . . perhaps he should go and say sorry. After all, that would be the grown up thing to do. As he approached her bedroom door, Tom could hear happy voices chattering away. He peeped in . . .

. . . and there was Katie surrounded by all her favourite toys and a delicious looking feast.

It looked like so much fun! There was plenty of toast with strawberry jam in front of Rosie Doll, and piles of dandelions for Rabbit. Teddy was munching on carrot sticks and Big Gorilla was eating a huge packet of jammy dodgers.

"But what did you need the socks for?" asked Tom curiously, peering round the door.

"They're for the sock monster of course!" said Katie, looking up at him and smiling. "He hasn't arrived yet but Mum says he lives in the washing machine. You can come in if you like!" she added. "If you're not too grown up for tea parties?"

"Oh I am!" replied Tom quickly. "Definitely." Then he had an idea. "But this isn't a tea party – this is a *feast*. In fact, it's a midnight feast! And I love midnight feasts. I know a few other people who love midnight feasts too . . ."

A few moments later Tom reappeared with his arms full. "This is Sergeant Sam," said Tom. "His favourite food is biscuits."

"Hello Sergeant Sam," said Katie politely. "Would you like a jammy dodger?"

"And this is Shark and Alien – they like carrot sticks and dandelions."
So Rabbit and Teddy shared with them. Fortunately Robot had brought his
own nuts to nibble on, so it didn't matter that Rosie had eaten most of the
toast already.

After they'd been playing for a while, Katie's tummy rumbled loudly.
"I know just the thing!" said Tom, and he ran along the hallway to his bedroom. He came back holding his special birthday chocolate bar. "You can't
have a midnight feast without chocolate," he said. Together they munched

down every last delicious crumb, and Tom decided that maybe baby sisters weren't so bad after all.

Later that night, when Mum popped her head around Katie's door, she was surprised to find the two of them snuggled up stickily together, fast asleep and surrounded by toys.

"Well I suppose I did tell them to play together." She smiled ruefully as she turned off the light and quietly pulled the door shut. "So I guess I'll have to wait until tomorrow to find out what they were doing with my socks!"

Happily
Ever After

Written by Amelia Hepworth

Illustrated by Natasha Rimmington

Happily Ever After

It was bedtime, and as usual Little Boo was enjoying her favourite bedtime story. " . . . and when the Big Bad Wolf had run away, Little Red Riding Hood and Granny lived happily ever after," said Daddy Bear. He softly closed the book and kissed Little Boo on the nose. "Goodnight and sleep tight," he smiled.

But this evening Little Boo was not sleepy – something was bothering her. She sat up on her pillow and gave Daddy back the book. "So what happened next?" said Boo. "Did the Wolf ever come back to the forest? Was he still hungry? Did he eat someone else instead?"

"No, no, no," said Daddy, "of course not!"

"Are you sure?" asked Boo in a worried voice.

"Yes, I'm sure," said Daddy, pausing for thought. "The Wolf went far away from the woods. And he lived happily ever after, too. Now go to sleep, Boo." Daddy Bear stood up slowly and gently tucked the blanket around Little Boo. But just as he was tiptoeing out of the room . . .

"How do you know?" asked Boo. "The Wolf might be living here. He might be outside my bedroom window!"

"The Wolf definitely isn't here. I know because . . ." Daddy Bear scratched his head for a moment . . . "because he went on holiday . . . to the beach. Wolves like a bit of sunshine every

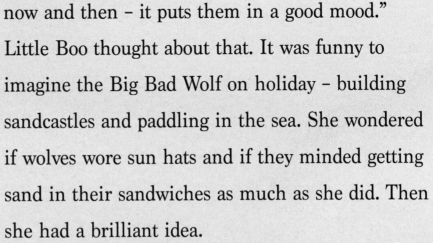

now and then – it puts them in a good mood." Little Boo thought about that. It was funny to imagine the Big Bad Wolf on holiday – building sandcastles and paddling in the sea. She wondered if wolves wore sun hats and if they minded getting sand in their sandwiches as much as she did. Then she had a brilliant idea.

"Can we go to the beach, Daddy?" she asked, bouncing around in her bed. "Maybe we'll see the Wolf! I wouldn't be scared if you were with me."

Daddy Bear laughed. "Silly Boo, it's bedtime!"

But Boo was already stuffing things into her rucksack. "Swim suit . . . sun hat . . . teddy . . . fishing net . . ." she mumbled as she packed. "Do you think the Wolf likes fishing, Daddy?"

"I think he prefers snorkelling actually," Daddy Bear said.

"Snorkelling is hard work!" said Boo seriously. "I think we'd better pack some sandwiches in case the Wolf gets hungry and tries to eat the children on the beach."

"Oh no, you don't need to worry about that!" said Daddy, sitting down on the bed. "The Wolf is perfectly safe. After he ran away from Little Red Riding Hood he became a vegetarian!"

Little Boo giggled. What a funny idea!

"And of course there are lots of other delicious things to eat at the beach," added Daddy, who was starting to enjoy himself.

"Like ice-cream?" asked Boo.

"Yes, and chips and candyfloss!" said Daddy.

"But not together," laughed Boo.

"Oh, definitely not," said Daddy.

"Still, I think we should probably make some sandwiches. Just in case," said Boo. So they went to the kitchen and made a huge stack of delicious jam sandwiches – two for each of them, and three for the Wolf.

Little Boo yawned as she packed them neatly away in her rucksack. "What else do we need?" she asked sleepily.

"Don't you think it's time for bed now, Boo?" asked Daddy gently. "We can go to the beach in the morning."

Little Boo thought about this. Perhaps it was a bit too dark for snorkelling. And the Wolf would probably be asleep right now. "OK. But can you tell me more about the Wolf please?"

"Then you promise to go to sleep?" sighed Daddy.

Boo nodded, and settled back down under the covers in her bed. So Daddy Bear told her all about the Wolf's holiday.

And about how the Wolf just happened to bump into the Three Little Pigs – who were also on their holidays – and how they made an enormous house out of sand together, and became firm friends. The Wolf even invited them to stay with him when they all got home!

"So you see," said Daddy, "the Wolf really is a reformed character, and he lived happily ever after. And now it really is time for bed."

But he needn't have worried . . . Little Boo was already fast asleep. Daddy Bear tiptoed over and gave her the softest goodnight kiss. "Sweet dreams," he whispered. "And happily ever after."

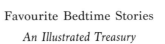

Favourite Bedtime Stories
An Illustrated Treasury

LITTLE TIGER PRESS LTD
an imprint of the Little Tiger Group
1 Coda Studios, 189 Munster Road,
London SW6 6AW
www.littletiger.co.uk

Published in Great Britain 2017
This volume copyright © Little Tiger Press 2016
Cover illustration by Jo Parry
Text and illustrations copyright © Little Tiger Press 2016

Printed in China
ISBN 978-1-84869-358-6
LTP/2700/1966/0917
2 4 6 8 10 9 7 5 3